THE CLIMB

AMRA PAJALIĆ

Content Warnings

SCAN QR CODE

OR GO TO

www.amrapajalic.com/themes.html

MELBOURNE, AUSTRALIA

https://www.pishukinpress.com/

Cover design: Created using Canva elements

Paperback Edition ISBN: 9781922871114

Chapter 1

'Hey Zephyra,' someone whispered behind her. She knew without turning around that it was Noah.

'What?' She turned slightly in her chair, still keeping her eyes on the whiteboard. Their English teacher was a hard nut and didn't appreciate chatting.

'Put your hand like this,' Noah said, demonstrating by holding his left elbow with his right hand.

She frowned, but complied. He looked at her chest and nodded.

Zephyra wanted to ask him what he was on about, but just then Ms Hardnut turned around and she quickly copied the last few sentences from the board. She had to wait ten minutes to have her curiosity satisfied when they were divided up in pairs.

'What was that about?' she asked Noah.

'I was doing the sag test,' Noah said.

Felicia, who was sitting behind them, looked horrified. She hunched in and tried to hide her boobs.

'What's the sag test?' Zephyra asked.

'It's where you check how far a girl's boobs are sagging and yours aren't sagging at all.' Noah looked at her chest and sighed wistfully.

If it was anyone else staring at her chest, she'd be creeped out, but this was Noah. They'd been best friends since year 7. He was like the younger brother she had never had.

'You're sick.' Zephyra smacked him in the chest. 'How would you like it if I wanted to measure if your nut sack was drooping?'

He leaned back in the chair and spread his legs. 'Measure away.'

'No thanks.' She looked away from his groin and flicked her hair. 'I don't want to see that. It's disgusting.'

'You're going to see one eventually,' Noah said, and closed his legs.

'No, I won't. I've seen enough.'

'Really? When did you see one?' he demanded.

At their first meeting during year 7 camp, he'd asked her out in a roundabout way. The teachers had devised a cunning plan to ensure students remained sleeping in their cabins at night. Every night after dinner, they took students for a one hour trek on the unsealed country streets until their feet ached from the gravelly road and their thigh muscles twitched. Getting into bed was a relief.

On their second night out, Noah broke away from his posse and stepped in beside Zephyra. Noah was tall and gangly like a bean pole, looming over a head taller than her, and he'd shortened his strides to match hers. Her friend picked up on his signal and sped up, leaving them to walk alone. After five minutes of small talk, he'd finally worked up the courage to pose his question.

'If a guy liked you and wanted to ask you out, would you say yes?'

'Even if a guy liked me, and I liked the guy who was asking me, I would say no because I'm not ready for a boyfriend,' she'd said.

'When are you going to be ready?' Noah had asked.

Since starting high school, it had seemed all everyone did was pair up and make out at lunchtime. It was like they were desperate to hurtle through this rite of passage of having their first boyfriend/girlfriend, so she wasn't surprised by the question.

'Maybe in year 10,' she'd said. She'd thought a lot on the subject. In the end she decided being 16 years old was a good age to have your first boyfriend. She wasn't eager to jump into her first relationship. While she'd had crushes, all of them were on boys who were older than her. Boys her age all seemed slightly gross and unkempt.

'Okay,' Noah had said, and returned to his posse.

After returning from camp, they drifted into friendship because they were in the same home group and both were outcasts. Noah was always slightly on the outside from the boys in his group; most of them viewed his height as a threat, and he drifted between hanging around with Zephyra and playing downball with year 10 boys. She didn't make many friends. She was a bookworm who enjoyed her character's inner lives more than those of her peers.

Once the possibility of an attraction or a relationship was off the table, they could become friends with none of the usual boy/girl pheromones interfering. Since then they'd never returned to the subject of us as a couple, but lately things were becoming weird.

'So when did you see a dick?' Noah demanded, bringing her back to the present.

'Shhh,' she hissed, looking around.

Felicia gave them another glare, but no one else seemed to have heard him.

'I watched that doco the other night,' she told Noah. 'You know the one about the guy and his sexual identity?' There had been a documentary on SBS that the entire school was buzzing about. This guy talked all about his sexual adventures. For the finale, he set up the camera and jumped out in front of it, stark naked, his flaccid penis wobbling about. She started laughing as she remembered. 'It was so hysterical the way it just wobbled there.' She looked up, expecting to see a smile on Noah's face, but he was dead serious.

'That's what happens,' Noah said. 'Dicks move about.'

'No, they don't,' she said. She'd read romance novels for years and all the penises mentioned were turgid.

'Yes, they do. They move. They're just like boobs. Soft and pliable.'

She looked at him, not sure whether he was having her on.

'What would you do if your boyfriend's dick did that?' he demanded, offended. 'Would you laugh at him?'

'I won't be having sex until I'm married,' she said.

Noah greeted her statement with stunned silence. 'What? You won't? Why not?' he finally demanded when his voice returned.

'Because I want to be in love and know that it's for real,' she said. 'He's going to be the only one.'

An unexpected gift that romance novels delivered was her resolve to remain a virgin until marriage. All the heroines in her romance novels were virgins and while the heroes might dally with women of easy virtue, he would only marry a woman who was 'pure.'

'Okay,' he said. 'What about your husband? Would you laugh at your husband like that?' He returned to the topic that had started this conversation, the dangling penis.

'I don't know.' She shrugged.

'I thought you were going to have a boyfriend in year 10?' Noah asked.

'Not anymore. I'm going to wait for my husband.'

'But how can you be sure that he's the one for you if you don't have sex before marriage?'

'I'll know,' she said.

She'd watched her mother's romantic misadventures and didn't see that there was anything to be gained by having sex before marriage. All of Mum's boyfriends seemed to change for the worst once she had sex with them. It was like once they realised she was in too deep and they could show their true nature. Zephyra would not let that happen. If a man loved her enough to wait for marriage, that meant he loved her for more than just sex.

Noah looked perplexed. Miss Hardnut called for attention.

'But do you expect your husband to be a virgin?' he whispered.

She shook her head. In all the romance novels, the hero wildly sowed his oats with different girls, and then when he met the heroine he settled for her, happy to be in a monogamous relationship for the rest of his life.

'I think a guy needs to experiment,' she said.

'Oh good,' Noah said. 'Anyway, it's probably best if one of you knows what to do in the bedroom.'

She gave him a dirty look. He turned to the board with a smirk.

Chapter 2

NOAH

After school, Noah waited by the gate for Zephyra. She saw him and smiled. They stepped in together, their routine as they lived close to each other.

They reached the milk bar. 'I'm going to buy a chocolate milk,' she said.

Noah nodded and waited outside, leaning on the wall. He was zoning out, living out his favourite fantasy where Zephyra realised they were meant to be together and they were kissing each other, her body pressed against his, when he saw Aaron Fenech and his gang approaching. Noah straightened from the wall, wiping the goofy smile off his face.

Fenech had it in for him since year 7 and took every chance to make his life hell.

'How's the game?' Noah asked Kenneth, a fellow student from his class.

Kenneth nodded and smiled, before noticing Fenech eyeballing him.

'What's it to you?' Fenech demanded, thrusting his chest toward Noah.

'Just asking,' Noah said, his mouth forming into an awkward smile.

'What did you say?' Fenech demanded. 'I didn't hear you.' He held up his hand to his ear.

Fenech was short, barely reaching Noah's nipples, and most of his mates were about his height. He seemed to find it an offence that Noah had started high school nearly at his full height of 190 centimetres.

Noah bowed his back and bent his knees, so that his head was closer to Fenech's. 'Just asking!' he repeated.

'That's right.' Fenech put his hand on Noah's neck. 'Bloody giraffe.' He pushed Noah, who stepped back. Fenech nodded at Kenneth, who elbowed Noah as he passed.

Noah hunched his shoulders and took it. He hated this part, where they descended into a mob mentality. They pushed him around like a fuse ball, before Fenech was satisfied he'd made his point and headed off.

'See you later, Jones,' Fenech called out of over his shoulder.

Kenneth met Noah's eyes, shaking his head sadly as he passed by. Noah knew he thought he should fight back, after all, they were like Oompa Loompas, but Kenneth wasn't the one stuck in this gangly body that made him a target. Noah had been taller than everyone else his whole life and all he'd ever wanted was to blend in and be one of the boys. If he fought and lost, it would never be the end of it.

Zephyra exited the milk bar. Noah watched the way she carefully inserted the straw into her chocolate milk. She stepped in beside him and said nothing as he straightened his shirt. He knew she saw, and scalding shame filled him. He hated that she saw him being a chickenshit. Everyone told him he should man up and smash the bastards. That would teach them a lesson. He fantasised about it every night before bed. The way he would smash Aaron Fenech's face. He was much taller than him, but Fenech was all muscle. He was on the footy team and was built like a tank. On the field, he didn't budge. Noah knew he didn't stand a chance against him. Fenech knew it too. The way he smirked at him, it was like he could read his mind. It wasn't just about tormenting him; it was knowing that he was full of rage, but couldn't do anything about it.

'See you tomorrow,' Zephyra said when she reached her street.

'See you,' Noah said.

Zephyra looked at him and hesitated. He knew she was debating whether to say something about the boys. *Please don't say anything,* he begged inside. He didn't want to see pity on her face.

'Mr Brent is organising a cycling fundraiser,' she said. 'I'm thinking of joining.'

'You are?' Noah said, keeping it cool.

He'd seen the flyers around the school. There were going to be training sessions twice a week riding bikes long distance, building up to a week of riding around the Murray River in male and female tours as a fundraiser for the food bank.

'What about you?' she asked.

His heart sped up as he thought about a week long camp with the two of them together. Anything could happen.

'I might do it too.'

She smiled and nodded.

He watched her walk away, allowing himself a minute to admire her curvy form. She was his dream girl with her hour-glass figure, dark wavy hair and brown eyes. He had to fight not to stare at her and could only steal glances when she was securely away from him. She turned to look over her shoulder and he waved, forcing his gaze away as he continued walking.

He felt lighter and full of hope. Maybe this was finally his chance to make a move. Ever since he started high school, she had been his one and only crush. He'd asked her out at a year 7 camp and she'd turned him down, saying she was waiting to have a boyfriend when she was older. At first, he thought she'd been just making up an excuse to reject him, like all the other girls he'd asked out. But he'd noticed on their return that she kept saying no to everyone. She wasn't interested in a boyfriend and so he became content to wait. He figured it was only a matter of time until she wanted someone and they could finally cross over from friends into something more. All he wanted was Zephyra.

He said he'd do the bicycle run, but there was only one problem. He entered the house and threw his backpack in the hallway.

'Dad,' he called out. He walked into the living room. Dad was standing above Mum. Mum was on the couch, her eyes red rimmed, a tissue against her face.

'What is it?' Dad asked.

'I was wondering if I could get a bike,' Noah said, finishing his train of thought as he processed what he was seeing.

'Why?' Dad asked.

Mum got up and left the living room.

'I'm wanting to do a bicycle tour,' Noah said. 'I'd have to train twice a week.'

'Good, good. It's just what I've been telling you. You need to build up some muscles.' Dad punched him on the arm, having to reach up as Noah loomed over him. He sat in the armchair. 'We'll go shopping on the weekend.'

Noah nodded. He went to his bedroom, passing the kitchen on the way. His Mum was standing over the sink, her hands soaking in the hot water. 'Mum,' he called to her.

Mum jerked.

'Are you okay?' Noah asked.

'Of course.' Mum forced a smile. 'It's just stupid hay fever.'

Noah hugged her. He got his height from his mum's side of the family and she was only ten centimetres shorter than him.

She patted his arm, leaving soapy bubbles. 'You're a good boy. Dinner will be ready in a little while. Grab a cupcake.'

Noah kissed her on the head and took a cupcake from the kitchen table. He was walking through the hallway when the phone rang.

He picked it up and said hello. There was silence. He said hello again. Mum appeared from the kitchen, wiping her hands on a tea towel. The person hung up and there was a dial tone in his ear.

'They hung up,' Noah said. Mum's face tightened with pain and she returned to the kitchen.

It was happening again. Noah bent over and unplugged the phone, hiding it so that it looked like the phone was still plugged in. He went to his bedroom. He couldn't believe that his dad was up to his old tricks. Last time he'd promised he'd never do it again. Noah remembered the shouting matches. He'd even woken during the night and seen Mum packing her bags, while Dad walked around begging her to give him a second chance. Afterward, everything settled down. Mum was cold toward Dad, but he was true to his word, coming home from work on time, bringing Mum flowers or a present. Taking her out to dinner. They even went away for a romantic weekend, leaving Noah and his sister with his grandfather. In the two years since, they were happy, and it was like it had never happened. Until now.

This was how it started last time. With phone calls that kept hanging up, and then a woman turned up on their doorstep to talk to Mum. Telling her she and Dad were in love. That Dad had promised they would be together. That he was unhappy in his marriage. Noah had snuck into his parent's bedroom and watched the woman leave from his parent's window that looked out onto the front. The woman was petite. Only 150 centimetres. She would have reached Dad's chest. Noah could just imagine how they would have fit together and the reason his dad was attracted to her.

Afterward, Noah heard Mum telling his sister, 'Never marry a man shorter than you.'

Noah didn't know what he felt. He was angry at his father for cheating on his mum and causing her pain, but he was also happy when Mum didn't leave. He didn't want to be the boy from the broken family.

He understood something about why his father did what he did. He had seen the same look that Fenech gave him when his dad looked at him. A look of resentment and anger. He wondered how much of this feeling was behind his father's infidelities.

Noah sat on the bed and put in his headphones as he fired up his game console.

'You there, Zephyra?' he called out.

'Online now,' Zephyra said, as she joined him.

He tuned out the world around him, Zephyra's voice in his headphones soothing him.

Chapter 3

Zephyra levelled up and killed Noah's avatar. 'Gotta go, have homework to do,' she told Noah.

'One more,' he pleaded into her headset.

'It's been an hour. We have English homework to do.'

'Don't care!'

She and Noah had different academic expectations: Zephyra was a straight-A student because of a combination of dogged work ethic and natural aptitude, while Noah suffered through school, struggling to concentrate and sit still for the allotted six hours of instruction, grazing the bottom of the achievement ladder. It was out of character from him not to respect her need to do homework.

'Is everything okay?' Zephyra asked, looking at his avatar on the screen.

Was he brooding about what happened with Fenech and his goons? The scenes of him being bullied were depressingly familiar. There was something about him being so tall that seemed to incite them—picking on Noah was a way of them proving their toughness.

She'd once attempted intervening. He'd looked at her with shame and embarrassment before running away. He'd avoided walking with her and they didn't speak for a month. Until the day she waited for him in front of his house in the morning and they walked to school together. They'd resumed their friendship as if nothing had happened. She'd learnt to hide and pretend she didn't see. It made it easier for both of them. But perhaps he wanted to talk about it now?

There was a pause, and she heard a deep intake of breath, as if he was about to speak. 'Nah, nothing I want to talk about. Later!' He hung up abruptly.

Zephyra took off her headset and gently placed it next to her console. She'd check in with him tomorrow, make sure he was alright.

She took out her notebook and soon zoned out as she drafted a practice essay for Macbeth. Her stomach rumbled, and she looked at the clock. It was six o'clock, time for dinner. She opened her bedroom door, her fists clenching as she heard her mother and her boyfriend Lee talking in the living room.

She opened the sliding door at the end of the hallway, quickly averting her eyes from the two of them wound together on the couch. Her mother didn't look up as she entered. Lee looked at her with a smirk, purposely putting his hand on her mother's butt and squeezing.

Zephyra scrunched her nose in disgust and went to the kitchen, making herself a sandwich and pouring orange juice. She walked past them and returned to the living room, keeping her eyes on the plate in her hand. Lee was the reason she was joining the cycling team and racing around the Murray. Spending hours sweating on a bike was better than enduring his presence at home.

She sat on her bed, placing her plate on the bedside table, and picked up the romance novel she'd been reading, feeling the familiar tropes of enemies to lovers soothing her. She ate her sandwich with one hand and held the book with the other, smiling as the hero and heroine engaged in banter and flirting.

This was the only romance she was interested in. Real life men and romance were nothing but drama and heartbreak. She'd seen that with her mother daisy-chaining from one boyfriend to another. Lee was the latest in a long chain, and one of the least tolerable ones, but the good news was that he would move on before long, undone by her mother's neediness and dramatics.

•••••••••••

The next day, Zephyra walked her bike to the front of the school. After the last bell, she'd changed into shorts and a t-shirt in the toilets, her helmet hanging off the handlebars. Noah careened next to her, hitting his brakes abruptly and skidding to a stop.

'Whaddya think?' he asked.

He was kitted out in lycra shorts and a t-shirt. The bike he was wheeling was shiny and top of the line.

'Wow, you went all out,' she said, glancing at her well-used bike she'd been riding since year 7.

'My dad took me shopping on the weekend. He insisted we get the most expensive one.'

He dismounted his bike and walked next to her. A shadow crossed his face. Maybe it wasn't Fenech that had been bothering him, but something at home.

'Is everything okay with your dad?' she asked.

He met her eyes quickly, his blue eyes shadowed with pain. He shrugged without speaking.

They'd been friends for too long. 'He's compensating, huh?' she breathed.

Noah nodded.

'I'm sure it will be okay.'

Noah swallowed. She put her arm around his waist, and they slowed their steps. She'd been side by side with Noah when his father was unfaithful to his mother the last time. They'd spent many hours on the phone or playing games while he drowned out his parents' arguing. Noah put his hand around her, pulling her to his side. She looked up at him and he pulled her tighter, so that they were pressed up against each other. His eyes were on her lips. *Oh, no, not again.*

'Your bike is a monster,' she said, stepping away from him and examining the handlebars.

He didn't respond. She felt his eyes on her face, attempting to cajole her to look at him. She thought they had established the parameters of their friendship in year 7, but Noah was trying to change the dynamic again. His arm on her back lingering a moment too long, the way he looked at her holding a little too much emotion. She was hoping he'd get the hint with no uncomfortable conversation.

'Yeah, Dad went all out,' he finally said, taking the hint.

She listened intently as he explained all the features. Other bike members slowly congregated in the carpark.

Mr Brent joined them and went over the safety features. She could feel Noah glancing at her throughout, but she ensured not to make eye contact with him. She was relieved to hit the open road and for the pain in her thighs and buttocks as they rode for an hour on the bike tracks of their suburb.

By the end of the session, they were all sweaty and sore. She struggled to ride home, Noah next to her.

'I'm dead.' She groaned as she dismounted in front of her house.

'That was absolutely awesome,' Noah said, smiling down at her as he circled her on his bike.

'Where do you get your energy from?' she asked, slugging back from her plastic bottle as she sat on the porch steps.

'Don't know. But I think I'm made for this.' Noah cycled hands free, his head back, a wide smile on his face.

She laughed, taking pleasure from his joy.

'I think I want to do extra training sessions this weekend. You in?' he asked.

Zephyra heard her mother and Lee inside her mother's bedroom, their sounds of pleasure carrying through the glass window, and shuddered.

'Yep, I'm definitely in,' she told Noah.

Chapter 4

NOAH

Zephyra sat on the picnic bench table that was perched on the hillside, her dark hair streaming behind her, the undulating hills of the national park forming a backdrop. He slowly undid his helmet, mesmerised by her joy. It was their second session in Brimbank Park, cycling up and down the walking and dirt tracks, developing their stamina.

'Isn't it a beautiful day to be out?' She spread her arms out and smiled.

'Every day with you is beautiful,' he said without thinking.

She looked at him; her smile fading.

He drew closer and sat next to her. 'Even when you're stinky from sweat,' he said, doing a fake sniff to break the tension.

She laughed, punching him in the arm. He sighed, fighting between the desire to make a move, and the fear that he should be patient and bide his time.

Zephyra took out the sandwiches she'd made from her backpack and handed him one.

'How are things with Lee and your mum?' he asked, biting into the ham and cheese sandwich she'd made for him, slathering it with mayo—just the way he liked it.

'She didn't hear from him for two days, so she rocked up at the nightclub that he's a bouncer at. Made a big scene about the waitress who works there.'

'So they broke up?' Noah asked.

'Nope. He loved it. He's been at our house for two days since. They haven't left the bedroom.'

'Sorry, didn't mean to put your off your food.' She still hadn't taken a bite of her sandwich.

'It's okay.' She took a bite. 'That's why I'm glad we're out here, listening to the sounds of nature.'

They ate in companionable silence for a few minutes.

Zephyra took a sip of her drink. 'What about your folks?' she asked.

Noah scrunched up this plastic bag and put it in her backpack. 'I almost wish they'd fight. It's like living in a tomb.'

Ever since the phone call hang ups and his mother's suspicion his father was having an affair again, his parents retreated into silence. They only spoke to each other when they absolutely had to, and then they were icily polite. Noah had woken up one night to get a snack and found his father snoring on the couch. He'd realised that his father slept on the couch every night, but woke up early and folded up his bedding, presenting the facade of a happy couple who still shared a bedroom.

'I'm sorry.' Zephyra took his hand in hers. He looked down and smiled, eating his sandwich one-handed as they held hands.

Zephyra blinked sleepily and yawned.

'Do you want to have a nap?' Noah opened his backpack and took out a blanket, which he laid out on the ground. He folded up his hoody and made it into a pillow before pulling her down, so they lay down next to each other, their heads sharing the hoody-pillow.

He looked up at the sky; the clouds drifting above them, peace descending on him. Zephyra's breathing deepened, and she curled against him. He put his arm under her head and curved his arm around her waist, joy dancing through him. She might not be willing to acknowledge her feelings while she was conscious, but as she slept she held him tightly, not letting him shift from her. He drifted into sleep too.

He felt Zephyra stir next to him and opened his eyes. She lifted her head and looked at him. He tucked her hair behind her ear and put his hand on the back of her head, pulling her down for a kiss.

Her eyes widened, and she jerked back. 'What are you doing?' She sat up, straightening her clothes.

'Doing a guy thing and trying to kiss a pretty girl,' he said, still lying on the ground, putting his arms behind his head. He felt too good and would not take her reaction as a rejection. While she slept, she'd revealed her true feelings. She trusted him completely. He just needed to stop trying so hard.

She looked at him, her mouth gaping open, before slapping his arm. 'Jerk.'

He said nothing, just smiled as he looked up at the sky. It was just a matter of time.

· · · ● · ● ● · · ·

Later, he rode Zephyra home and stopped at the milk bar to buy a Gatorade. When he stepped out, he saw Aaron Fenech and his mates looking at his bike.

'We thought it was you, Jones,' Fenech said as he looked him up and down in his lycra shorts and t-shirt. 'Don't you look stylish?'

'Thanks,' Noah said, getting sick of his jibes. He reached for his handlebars, but Fenech's hands were on it, preventing him from pulling the bike away from the wall.

'What's your hurry?' Fenech asked.

'I have to get home,' Noah said, not letting go. He still felt the usual terror and panic in his stomach, but something was different. He was suddenly sick of Fenech's bullshit. His jibes and bullying. Standing so close together, Noah was aware of how much taller he was. Since he'd been training, he'd filled out. He didn't need to do anything about his legs. The cycling took care of that, but he'd been doing weights and sit-ups to develop his torso. He needed to carry the bike over rough terrain and absorb the shocks of the handlebar. Standing so close to

Fenech, he realised he was almost as wide as him. While he didn't have Fenech's bulkiness, he had height.

Fenech realised it, too. There was a moment of discomfort in his face when Noah didn't back down. Fenech had to decide whether to back down and step away or keep the confrontation going.

Fenech let go of the handlebars. Noah swung his leg over the seat and was about to swing off.

'Look at that,' Fenech said, smirking as he looked around at his posse. 'Jones here is shaving his legs. Are you wanting to be more attractive to your boyfriend?'

Noah looked at him with annoyance. 'All cyclists shave their legs.'

Fenech looked surprised. He'd obviously expected that this would get under Noah's skin, and he didn't know what to say.

'Really, I thought it was only poofs.'

'So you're calling all cyclists poofs, including Randy?' Noah asked, mentioning Fenech's younger brother, who was also on the team.

'Hey, leave him out of this,' Fenech said, pushing his chest toward Noah.

'You're the one who brought it up,' Noah said.

'Don't you call my brother a poof,' Fenech said.

'I'm not,' Noah said. 'You did that.'

Fenech's eyes widened. He was shocked Noah was talking back.

'I didn't call Rodney a poof. I called you a poof,' Fenech yelled.

Noah was on the street, about to push off on his bike. He could pretend that he hadn't heard what Fenech said and just ride off. But without even knowing he was going to do it, he dropped the bike onto the ground and headed back.

Fenech's eyes widened when he saw Noah walking back towards him. Noah saw in slow motion Fenech's arm swinging back for a punch. Noah moved slightly to the right and Fenech's punch connected with his shoulder instead of his face.

Noah lifted his arm and formed a fist. He aimed it at Fenech, putting his whole body behind it. His fist connected, Fenech's face crumpling like a deflated ball under the force. Fenech's head snapped back. Noah didn't give him a chance to recover. His rage unleashed, he kept punching. Some of his punches connected, some didn't, but the force of them kept Fenech from being able to do anything more than flinch. With his greater height, Noah had greater reach to hit at Fenech, but Fenech couldn't hit him back. His shorter arms fell just short, and when he connected with Noah, it was weak and barely stopped Noah's assault.

Noah's fist connected with Fenech's nose, and blood spurted out. Fenech fell backwards, his hands covering his nose and mouth. Noah had his arm up, fist formed, ready to punch again, but seeing the way Fenech flinched brought him back to his senses.

He looked at Fenech's two mates. They avoided his gaze and stepped back.

Noah stopped, taking deep breaths.

He knew this was where he should say something. Make some big announcement about Fenech watching his step and staying away from him, but his whole body was shaking. He knew he had to get out of there before the adrenaline wore off and he became a blubbering mess.

Noah turned and got on his bike, riding away without looking back. He rode furiously, glad to have an outlet for his crazy energy. He couldn't go home so keyed up. His parents would want to know what happened, and Dad couldn't find out. It was his dad who had taught him to be a mouse and let the bullies win.

They'd been to a footy game and were exiting when a Hawthorne supporter started up. 'Take that shirt off, you loser,' he shouted as Noah and his Dad walked past.

His Dad just walked by, pretending he didn't hear him, but the Hawthorne supporter wasn't backing down.

'Did you hear me?' he'd demanded, stepping into Dad's way and tugging on his Dad's Western Bulldogs shirt.

His Dad pushed him away and the Hawthorn supporter chest bumped him. 'You heard me,' he said menacingly.

'I want no trouble,' Dad had said.

'Is that right?' He'd flicked Dad's Western Bulldogs hat off. 'Then take it off.'

Dad had looked down at the ground as he took off his shirt.

'Drop it,' the Hawthorne supporter ordered.

Dad had dropped it onto the ground. As Noah watched, the man stepped on the shirt and ground it into the dirt.

Dad had hunched and side-stepped the man.

The man let him go.

'But Dad, what about your hat and shirt?' Noah had asked.

'Leave it,' his dad had said, grabbing hold of his arm and pulling him along.

That was the moment Noah had learnt to avoid a fight at whatever cost. And that's why he knew he couldn't go home while he was so keyed up after the fight. Things had been weird between him and Dad since he'd shot up. He didn't know how Dad would take it if he knew he'd taken on a bully and won. There was only one person who he could tell. He swerved right and headed to Zephyra's house.

He knocked on the door, and she answered.

'What's wrong?' she asked as soon as she saw his bloody top.

'Yeah, I need to talk to you.'

She stepped out of the house and walked with him on the porch. There was a chair and a table set. He leaned on the porch fence.

'I had my first punch up,' Noah said, glancing at her quickly.

'Are you all right?' she asked, looking him up and down. 'Did you get hurt?' She reached for his arm and peered into his face.

'Nah, you should see the other guy,' he said, his voice cracking. 'I won the fight.'

He still couldn't believe it. He'd spent years fantasising about smashing Fenech's face. Every time he'd imagined it, he'd been full of satisfaction and joy, but now all he felt was guilt as he imagined the pain on his face.

'I smashed Fenech in the face,' Noah said.

'You did?' Zephyra's voice was full of disbelief.

He saw himself through her eyes. The gangly, awkward boy who was always so unco. He wanted to prove himself to her.

'Yeah, I reckon I broke his nose,' he boasted.

Zephyra's eyes widened. 'Shit, do you think he'll go to the police?'

For a moment, pure fear filled him, then he thought it through. There was no way Fenech was going to dibber dobber. Losing a fight was bad enough, but going to the cops would bottom out any integrity he had as a hard man.

'Nah.'

'What happened?' Zephyra asked.

'He was giving me shit as usual, but suddenly I wasn't going to take it anymore. I'm not going to be anyone's bitch.'

As he said it, he realised what had changed. He'd spent so much time fearing the pain of a punch up, but while training in bike riding, he'd experienced lots of pain and it hadn't killed him. He had a high pain threshold. It suddenly seemed absurd that he had ever feared Fenech and a punch from him. That he had played the monkey in order to avoid it. Fury filled him.

'No one's ever going to fuck with me again,' he said.

Zephyra looked at him with concern. 'Okay.'

She didn't look like she believed him. In her eyes he was still unco Noah. He suddenly didn't want to stay and talk to her. It just pissed him off. He didn't know what he'd expected. For her to fall into his arms like he was a hero, but she was just looking at him in the usual way. He felt so different, but she saw nothing.

'Anyway, I have to get going.' He headed down the stairs.

'Noah, Noah,' she called his name as she followed him. She grabbed his arm. He stopped.

'I'm just glad you weren't hurt.'

He looked at her. With him on the bottom stair, their faces were close together. He looked at her lips and leaned in to kiss her. His lips brushed hers, when she snapped her head back.

'What was that?' she asked.

'You know what that was,' Noah said, suddenly sick of the bullshit.

'You know how I feel about you,' Zephyra said. 'You're my friend.'

'I'm just a friend, but I'm not boyfriend material.'

'That's not what I said.'

'No, you didn't have to.' Noah turned back and stepped down. He got on his bike and rode away.

There was a tearing in his chest and the wind dried his tears as he rode. He'd thought that when he won his first fight, things would change, but they didn't. He was still the same guy, and Zephyra would never see him as anything different.

Chapter 5

Zephyra walked out of her house to find her street empty. Usually, Noah was waiting for her to walk to school together. Why must he be such a boy? They were friends, nothing more!

In class, he was sitting at the front, next to Felicia and some other girls. He saw her enter and turned his head away. Zephyra huffed as she went to their usual seats in the back. At recess, she went to his locker, hoping to clear the air, but a rag-tag group of girls and boys surrounded him. He was not hanging around in his usual crowd. Noah had moved up in the world.

'I punched Fenech's nose and his blood spurted like a fountain. The bastard screamed and ran away.' Noah regaled his audience, reenacting the fight. Everyone watched him in awe.

He looked at her, briefly making eye contact, snubbing her as he returned his attention to his posse. She fumed. Was he really going to be this immature?

By lunchtime she'd had enough and she ducked into the library and slid into the world of her romance novel. There was no disappointment or surprise in her book.

As she walked home, Zephyra saw him ahead of her, with his new crowd. She slowed her steps, letting them move ahead of her. She'd always been honest with him. He knew she liked him as a friend, and nothing more, but still he kept trying. And now he was acting like he was the victim.

A crowd of people shouted and yelled as she walked through the park. Noah yelled. She pushed through the crowd, horror filing her as she saw Noah being held up by two big men, as Fenech punched him in the gut. Noah doubled over, his legs not touching the ground as he hung in the air.

She looked around, expecting someone to step in and help Noah, but they were all enjoying the spectacle.

Fenech pulled his arm back, going to punch Noah again.

'Stop it, you coward,' Zephyra shouted, yanking Fenech's arm back. It was like pushing a Mack truck. He didn't move.

Noah lifted his head, looked at her with surprise.

Fenech shook her off, and she fell to the ground. Noah roared, tearing himself away from his captors. He threw a wild punch, connecting to the ear of one man, and headed for Fenech. The other guy grabbed him by the waist and tugged him back.

Fenech smiled as he headed for Noah, who was now on his knees, wrestling to get free. Fenech pulled back his fist, ready to smash Noah in the face. Zephyra's hand touched a rock, and she stood, hitting Fenech on the back of the head with the rock. Fenech looked at her with surprise before falling over. His mates dropped Noah, who fell on all fours to the ground. Fenech's mate reached for her. Zephyra swung the rock, hitting one of them with a glancing blow on the shoulder. The other one yanked the rock from her hand, holding her arms to her torso.

The other mate lifted Fenech off the ground, who looked dazed. Blood dripping on his forehead.

'That little bitch,' Fenech muttered, looking in her direction. Fenech headed for her, his fist raised.

'Leave her alone,' Noah shouted, throwing himself forward and knocking Fenech over. The mate holding Zephyra let go and they were all tangled with Noah. Zephyra found the rock again and hit the huddle, hitting Fenech's mate in the back.

The police siren sounded close, and the crowd dispersed. Fenech's mates looked up, catching the sight of the police car and ran, leaving Fenech on the ground by himself. Noah pushed Fenech off, knelt on his knees before her.

'Are you okay?' he asked, his hands caressing her arms as he checked for injuries.

'I'm fine,' Zephyra said, breathlessly. She took stock of her injuries. There were a few sore spots on her torso from loose limbs connecting during the melee and her upper arms hurt where they'd held her down, but she was okay. She dropped the rock she was holding.

'What were you thinking?' Noah demanded, tears in his eyes. 'They could have hurt you.'

'So could you,' she shouted. Adrenaline was wearing off, and she was trembling all over.

'I'm a guy. I can take it,' Noah said gruffly.

'I'm a girl. I can take it too.'

They eyeballed each other for a moment, before Noah hugged her, his head pressed against her torso. 'I couldn't live with myself if anything happened to you.'

'And I can't take you being hurt.' She cupped his head and hugged him back.

Two police officers were walking toward them. Fenech saw them and attempted to stand, but his eyes looked unfocused. There was blood streaming down his ear. She hoped she hadn't given him a concussion.

The crowd had dispersed and the three of them were the last ones left. 'We received a complaint that there was a physical altercation in progress,' the red-headed constable said, when he'd reached them.

Noah stood, putting his arm around his shoulders. The second constable, a blonde woman, approached Fenech and helped him stand. 'You might need a doctor, mate.'

'Nah, I'm good.' Fenech stepped away from the blonde constable.

'So what happened here?' The redhead asked.

Fenech looked too dazed to speak.

'He fell,' Noah said.

The blonde constable picked up the rock next to Zephyra, blood on it. 'Are you sure about that?' she stared at Noah.

'Ask him?' Noah nodded to Fenech.

'Yeah, I fell. I fell,' Fenech interjected.

The Constables split them up, trying to get to the true story, but they stuck to the cover. The Constables took down their names and contact details.

'Do you want us to drive you home?' they asked Fenech.

Fenech looked wildly at Noah, terrified at the thought of being driven home in a police car.

'Nah, I'll walk him home.' Noah approached Fenech and put his arm around his shoulders. 'I'll make sure he gets there safely.'

Zephyra heard the relish in his tone, as did Fenech, who winced at Noah's emphasis on safe.

The Constables left the park and returned to their police car and she stepped in beside Noah, who was still hugging Fenech.

'Get off me,' Fenech muttered, trying to shrug Noah off.

'Take it easy, mate.' Noah patted his back and forced a laugh. 'We don't want the nice police officers to think anything is wrong now, do we?'

The Constables sat in the car and by the time they'd reached the street; they drove off.

They reached an alley beside the park. 'You wait here, Zephyra,' Noah said, and frog-marched Fenech down the alley.

Zephyra turned her back in the alley, looking out toward the street. She heard a guttural moan and Noah's muttering under his breath. He returned, sans Fenech.

'Fenech has decided to walk home by himself.'

Zephyra looked behind worriedly. 'What if he's got a concussion? I could be up for charges if something happens to him.'

Noah stopped, staring at the sky as he took a deep breath. He took out his phone. 'Randy, your brother is in the alley next to Bletchley Park. He needs you to come pick him up.'

'What happened?' she heard Randy ask.

'He fucked with the wrong person.' Noah hung up and hugged her shoulders, turning them toward their homes. 'Are you sure you're alright?'

Zephyra nodded. Now that it was over, she suddenly felt exhausted. She couldn't wait to get home and sleep. She leaned against Noah and they walked together.

'I can't believe you jumped in like that,' Noah said, kissing her head.

'Of course. You're my best friend.' She wrapped her arms around his waist and enjoyed the sensation of him helping her walk.

'I'm sorry for being a jerk,' Noah said. 'I just like you—'

'I like you too. You're my best friend,' she interrupted him.

Noah sighed, rubbing her back. 'Yeah, you're my best friend, too.'

He walked her to her door and unlocked it for her. Helped her to her bed, taking off her shoes while she sat on the edge. She lay down with a sigh, feeling him covering her with a blanket as she drifted into sleep.

Chapter 6

NOAH

'Here's your sleeping bag,' his mum entered, holding the green nylon sleeping bag in her hands.

'Thanks.' Noah took it and placed it next to the backpack he was packing for the competition.

'Did you prepare a list of what to pack?' his mother asked.

Noah shook his hand, blowing out a sigh and making his fringe flop onto his forehead. Mum handed him a sheet. He looked at it and saw she'd prepared a list.

'Thanks Mum.' He kissed her on the cheek, before tipping out the contents of his backpack and beginning packing again, this time ticking off the list.

'Are you excited?' she asked.

He nodded, ticking off the t-shirts.

'You and Zephyra are going to be alone for a week.'

Noah's cheeks flushed. He'd been thinking about that a lot more than he should have. Over the past two months of training, they'd spent most of the week together after school, training twice a week with Mr Brent and then going for a long bike ride through Brimbank Park and the surrounding suburbs. They'd always take a picnic and stop in the park, chill and hang out. Ever since the day of the fight, he'd realised she felt more for him than she wanted to admit. Since then, their friendship had been slowly inching to the next level as he stopped trying to force anything. This weekend, they would camp together. They would be beneath the stars every night, side by side. This was his chance for her to admit her feelings and that they were more than just friends.

'Just remember, if you do anything, use protection.' His Mum handed him a box of condoms.

He flushed bright red.

'I'm not kidding. Make sure you use protection every single time.' His mother tilted his face down to look at her.

He knew where her concern was coming from. His parents got married six months after he was born. He knew from his grandfather's muttering that his parents had a shotgun wedding.

Noah nodded, quickly taking the condoms and stuffing them in the front pocket of his backpack.

'Good boy.' His mother kissed his cheek and left.

Noah sat on the edge of his bed, the condoms taunting him. He knew his mother was taking care of him, but he wished she hadn't given them. Now he could think of nothing else. The most he had imagined was him and Zephyra kissing, now that he had the condoms, his fantasies were unfurling more and more.

He finished packing and took a photo, sending it to Zephyra. 'Ready for tomorrow.'

She sent him a photo back of her backpack and sleeping bag.

'Me too.'

He lay back in bed, smiling as he thought about their weekend together. He was watching videos on his phone when he received a message from Zephyra. 'Might not be going,' she said. 'Lee and Mum broke up.'

Shit! Noah jackknifed out of bed, pacing up and down. He desperately wanted Zephyra to come with him. This was his one chance to spend more time together, but he knew what her relationship with her mother was like. Whenever her mother was single, she leaned on Zephyra for moral support, needing her to spend time with her as she licked her wounds. Zephyra always put her life on hold.

He started typing a message, telling her to choose herself, was about to hit send, but couldn't do it. He took a photo of him looking sad and sent it to her with the caption. 'I understand.'

She sent him back a sad photo of herself.

'Do you want me to come over?' he asked.

He watched the three dots on the message as she typed, holding his breath as he waited.

'Yes,' she replied.

He ran out the door. 'Going to see Zephyra,' he yelled at his mother. He jumped on his bike and pedalled to Zephyra's house.

She was sitting on the porch waiting for him, wearing a red cardigan over her cat pyjamas.

'How's your mother?' he asked as he leaned his bike against her house.

'She's tired herself out with her crying.'

He sat on the porch next to her. It was a coolish night, and she shivered. 'You should get dressed,' he said, touching her cold feet.

'I don't want to go in there.' She sounded so defeated and tired.

'Alright then.' He took her feet and placed them on his lap, tucking them into his hoody.

'Thanks,' she said and leaned against his shoulder. 'I'm so tired of her drama. She keeps jumping from relationship to relationship and it's always the same: the declarations of undying love, the never-ending passion, the jealousy and possessiveness that drives them away, and then the messy break up and recovery.'

'Yeah, you'd think that they would act more mature as they get older,' Noah said. Over the past few months, his father had placated his mother, denying that he'd had another affair. That it was just a crank caller. His mother seemed to have bought his act, but Noah wasn't too sure. 'You know, when Dad picked me up from footy training a few weeks ago, I smelt perfume in the car.'

'I'm so sorry.' Zephyra hugged him, and he placed his arm around her.

Noah leaned his chin on her head, inhaling the smell of rose shampoo. He looked down at her, fantasising about lifting her head up so that they looked at each other and kissed. He shook himself out of his daydream. Now wasn't the time.

He took a deep breath, looking out onto the street before him. 'That's one reason I'm looking forward to a week around the Murray. I don't have to think about all their drama.'

'That's the dream. A week without drama.'

'I mean… it could be. All you have to do is come to school tomorrow.'

She groaned, hiding her face in his chest. 'I know. I wish I could just leave her.'

He looked down at her, his heart hurting at the feelings rising before him. 'Then you wouldn't be the Zephyra I know and love.' His muscles tensed, hoping she wouldn't react to his almost declaration of love.

'I'm so lucky to have a best friend like you.' She lifted her face toward him, tears glistening on her eyelashes.

He was caught between warring instincts: one part of him desperately wanted to lean down, to kiss her, the other, more rational part was fixated on her use of 'best friend.' Was that all he was to her? Just a friend. He'd thought they were inching closer to transitioning into something more.

There was a bang from inside the house, and Zephyra jerked back. 'She's awake. I'd better go in.'

He took her feet out from his jumper and stood. She tried standing up and wobbled, and he steadied her, pulling her into him and almost lifting her off her feet.

'Damn, you've really filled out.' She caressed his chest and his arms. 'You're like a super hunk now.' Her eyes were wide with wonder.

He started leaning down. Stuff it. It was now or never. The front door slammed open behind them and her mother stood in the doorway, her hair disheveled, her eyes red-rimmed.

'Let's do a fast food run.' She jangled her keys.

He reluctantly took his hands off her.

'Okay, Mum.' Zephyra stepped back. 'Good luck for tomorrow.' She stood on tip-toe and kissed him, before walking toward the car with her mum.

He got his bike and pedalled behind them as they drove down the street. They turned left at the end of the street, and he turned right. It would be okay. They were only going to be apart for a week. And then he'd make his big move.

Chapter 7

Zephyra woke on the couch in the living room. She lay there with her eyes closed, hearing a murmur of voices. She fluttered her eyelashes open and saw her mother and Lee kissing in the doorway.

'I'm sorry baby,' Mum was muttering between kisses, her hands on his back. 'I missed you so much.'

'I'm glad you called,' Lee said, pushing her against the wall and grinding his hips against her.

Zephyra closed her eyes, pretending to sleep.

'Let's go to my bedroom.' Her mother led Lee down the hallway.

Zephyra turned on her back and stared at the ceiling, disappointment welling inside her. She'd stayed up until two in the morning, comforting her mother after her brutal break up. Her mother had promised that she was done with Lee and his shady ways. He was unreliable and wouldn't ever meet her plans. When he showed up he was always hours later, and then would ghost her for days at a time. Her mother was constantly at his beck and call.

Zephyra had been willing to give up all her plans to be there for her mother, and as soon as she was asleep, she called Lee for a booty call. She looked at the clock. It was five o'clock.

It wasn't too late.

Zephyra went to her room. She hadn't un-packed her backpack. She re-checked all her goods. Went to the kitchen and made sand-wiches and prepared snacks for the bus trip. At seven o'clock, as the sun was rising, she left her house, carrying her backpack and sleeping bag to the bike. She'd left a note for her mother telling she was going on the trip.

She waited outside of Noah's house. At seven on the dot, he stepped out of his house wearing his lycra outfit. In the two months they had been riding, climbing up and down the hills and valleys of Brimbank Park, he had become toned and filled out. The bike naturally toned the legs and thighs, and Noah had been doing weights for his upper body. He looked, well... not like Noah. If he wasn't her best friend, she'd have to say that he was hot.

He saw her and beamed, running toward her like an exuberant puppy. This was the Noah she knew. Slightly goofy and fun. He hugged her tightly. 'You're coming!'

'Yep. Mum backslid with Lee and I don't want to deal with that drama.' Pressed up against him, she was aware of how solid and large he felt. What was happening to her?

Noah looked down at her, and she saw his eyes shift to her lips. *Oh, no, what was he thinking?* His father came out the front door and Noah turned toward him.

'Zephyra is coming!' he shouted triumphantly.

'I'm so glad,' his dad said. 'It devastated Noah that you weren't going.'

Devastated, such a strong word.

'We'd better get going.' Noah strapped on his helmet. 'We have to be at school in half an hour.' He hugged his father and got on the bike.

As she rode behind him, Zephyra kept glancing at his broad back. Where he could, Noah rode beside her, a beaming smile on his face. Zephyra was happy to meet her goal of completing the marathon. And she was happy to be spending time with Noah, but now she was wondering if this was such a good idea. In the past, when emotions got too heated, or she felt he was becoming too strong with his affections, she could always leave and go home. Now they were going to be joined at the hip for the next week. Maybe this wasn't her greatest idea! No, she needed to stop worrying. She and Noah were best friends, nothing more, and he knew that. And besides, they'd be exhausted after riding for hours. There wouldn't be much time or energy for mucking around.

At the school Noah helped Mr Brent place the bicycles and backpacks of those travelling onto the trailer, before they got on the bus. They'd begun with 15 students taking part. Over the past two months, the numbers had whittled down until there were only eight of them left with Mr Brent.

She followed Noah on and toward the back of the bus, away from everyone else. As they walked down, Felicia hungrily looked at Noah as he passed, taking in the sight of him in his lycra outfit, outlining his every bicep and sinew. That was new. Zephyra hadn't seen Noah as a desirable male until now. She wasn't the only one who had noticed Noah's slamming body. Maybe this was just normal.

Noah moved up and let her take the window seat, before sitting on the aisle.

'You should have seen the look Felicia gave you,' she whispered again in his ear when he sat down.

He looked at Felicia in bewilderment.

'She looked like she wanted to eat you.'

He smiled shyly, his cheeks flushing, and looked down at his lap.

'Are you feeling bashful about being desired, Monsieur Jones?'

Noah looked at his hands, his cheeks flushing even more. 'You'd better get used to it, Mr Muscles.' She placed her hand on his chest, meaning to slap him like a mate, but somehow her hand softened, gently caressing his bicep.

Noah met her eyes, his pupils darkening with desire. She went to remove her hand, but he held it down, pushing it against him. He leaned down, angling his head toward her lips. She froze.

'Ladies and Gentlemen,' Mr Brent called from the front, giving them up a much needed interruption.

Noah reluctantly let go of her hand, and they looked to the front. Zephyra's breathing was rapid, her heartbeat fluttering. What the hell was that? Instead of moving away, she'd almost wanted him to kiss her. What was wrong with her?

After Mr Brent gave them the overview of the trip and the rules, Zephyra took out her banana. 'Haven't had breakfast,' she lied, shoving it in her mouth, giving herself a much-needed distraction and a buffer in case Noah was thinking about pursuing the kiss again.

He nodded. Soon the bus was on the freeway, and the lull of its motion made her eyes flutter. She yawned, covering her mouth. 'Sorry. I'm so tired.' She'd only caught a few hours of sleep early in the morning.

'Sleep now.' Noah lay his head back and closed his eyes. 'When we stop, we're going to be pedalling hard.'

Zephyra nodded, closing her eyes too. She didn't know how long she slept for, but when she woke up, she was draped across Noah's chest. He was cradling her against him, their chests pressed up against each other, she almost on his lap. As her eyes fluttered open, she saw his face above hers. It took her a moment to orientate herself. As he leaned down, she jerked up, hitting into something hard with her buttocks.

Noah yelped, his hands reaching for his crotch. As she scrambled onto her seat, she saw he was clutching his erection. She'd slammed into it as she tried to escape his pass.

'Everything alright back there,' Mr Brent called, as all heads turned towards them.

Zephyra flushed with embarrassment, hiding her face behind the seat in front of her.

'Just hit my leg,' Noah lied through gritted teeth, taking his hands off his crotch and placing them on the handset.

She quickly glanced down and saw the erection was gone.

She glanced across the aisle and saw Terry ogling them and quickly ducked back behind Noah's shoulder so she wouldn't see him. This was so embarrassing. What if he told people about Noah's erection? What if people wondered what they were doing at the back for him to get an erection? How could he have done this to her?

She clenched her hands into fists as rage built within her. This was his fault. How the hell did she end up across his lap? Damn him.

Chapter 8

NOAH

Noah got up first and let Zephyra pass. He waited in the aisle as the bus emptied. She didn't look at him once as she passed. He knew by the straight posture of her back that she was pissed. Shit. He kicked the bus seat. This was supposed to be his big moment, and he'd fucked everything up.

They'd both fallen asleep, and he'd woken to find her leaning against his shoulder. He'd watched her sleeping, his hopes lifting at the thought of the holiday. As she descended deeper into sleep, her head started flopping forward so he'd hugged her, holding her more against him. And somehow, she'd ended up lying across him. Looking down at her, he'd been able to see her breasts bobbing with each bump in the road, and as he did, his desire rose. He'd gotten turned on and had tried squirming, making it go away. Noah had fought not to look, but his eyes just kept returning. He'd held her tightly, waiting for her to wake up so that they could continue their kiss.

When she woke for a moment, it had seemed it would be perfect. She'd looked at him with such a sweet smile and he'd thought this was it. He'd leaned down, only for everything to explode at once. He couldn't get the image of her horrified face when she caught sight of his erection, or the throbbing in his balls from her knee.

He plodded out of the bus. 'You okay, Jones?' Mr Brent asked when he stepped out.

Noah nodded despondently.

'It happens. You're a young man.' He clapped him on the shoulder.

Noah realised that Mr Brent knew what had happened. Horror filled him and he looked at his peers. They were watching him and snickering. They all knew. Damn Terry and his big mouth. He glanced at Zephyra. She gave him a death stare and snapped her neck in the opposite direction, flicking her hair.

'Let's get everything unpacked, Jones,' Mr Brent called.

Noah nodded and followed him to the trailer, relieved to have something to occupy his hands. After they'd emptied the trailer, the students congregated at the park that the organisers had set up as the start arena. There were nearly a hundred participants, at least a quarter of young students, while the rest were adults. Noah remained on the perimeter of the group. He needed to give Zephyra a chance to calm down. Hopefully, by the time they completed the first stage of a four-hour ride, she'd be calmer and willing to hear his apology.

'Do you want some sunscreen?' Felicia held out a bottle.

He nodded. He squirted it into his hand, rubbed it on his face.

'Don't forget your ears.' She approached, rubbing the sunscreen onto the top of his ears.

She was much smaller than him and as she arched to reach his ears, her boobs arched into his chest. He felt himself harden. *Oh, no, not again.*

Felicia bounced against him more, her hand descending to his arm. 'Here, you need to rub some on your arms too.'

He looked down at her. She was rubbing sunscreen on his bicep, her tongue on her lip, her breasts jiggling. She met his eyes and leaned against him. His erection was unmistakable against her, but she didn't flinch. She smiled and her eyes became heavy-lidded. Was she enjoying it?

'Here, can you hold my jacket?' She tossed her jacket onto his lap, hiding his erection, before bending to return the sunscreen into her backpack. God, it was too much. He looked out into the distance, thinking about the most disgusting images he could pull forth from his memory: the time he had diarrhoea, cleaning the chicken pen at his grandparent's house, the rotten meat in the freezer he had to clean—trying to force his dick back to behaving.

When he felt it had worked, he lifted the jacket. 'Here you go.'

Felicia took it with a conspirator smile. They were in on it together. He sat on his bike, desperate for the ride to begin. He looked ahead and saw Zephyra watching him, giving him the death stare again. At this rate, he wouldn't get out of her bad books soon.

He was relieved when the whistle blew, and they all began riding. The wind against his body, his legs pumping as his bike climbed up hill, the air pushing through his lungs. Soon he was lost in the rhythm of his body and everything else fell away.

When they finished the ride four hours later, he was bathed in sweat, his legs feeling like jello, an invincible feeling in his body. His dick wouldn't be giving him any trouble after that hard ride.

He milled around as the judges collated the rankings. They were camping near a caravan park. Noah set up his tent in record time, knowing that once he had a shower, he wouldn't have energy for anything else. He took out Zephyra's tent and placed it next to him. They had agreed to place their tents together so they could spend time together.

He was just finishing when she pulled up. 'Perfect timing.' He stepped back, admiring their two tents.

'Oh, great.'

Zephyra put her bike next to his, fiddling with her kickstand. Shit, should he talk about before or pretend it didn't happen?

'Listen, about before—'

'Going to have a shower.' She cut him off, taking her backpack and hotfooting it to the shower block at the caravan park.

So they were going to pretend then. Shit, it was going to be a long night. He went to the shower block and returned, but Zephyra was still missing in action.

'You going for dinner?' Felicia walked up to him, her hair wet, smelling of something citrusy.

'I was going to wait for Zephyra,' Noah said.

'She's still in the shower. She can meet us there.' Felicia hooked her arm through his and led him toward the mess hall and the barbecue.

His stomach rumbled as they got closer, the sausages filling the night air.

'Man, my butt hurts.' Felicia cupped her butt and massaged it as they walked. 'I thought I'd prepared enough, but I'm still sore. What about you?'

'I'm okay.' He was feeling pretty good. While he was tired, it was that tiredness that came from achieving something good. He felt calm and peaceful. The only throbbing he was feeling was in his groin, which was soothed after some self-love in the shower.

He piled his plate high and joined the table where his school teammates were. Felicia sat next to him and they talked over dinner, everyone sharing their best moments from the ride.

He saw Zephyra arrive at the end. She took a plate and disappeared back into the darkness. He felt a thickness in his throat, swallowing hard as he realised she was avoiding him. Had he done something so unforgivable that she couldn't even look at him? Felicia laughed next to him, looking up at him, her eyes shining from the lights. Felicia wasn't treating him like a pariah. She was still behaving like normal. He tried to push Zephyra from his mind.

When he went to his tent, hers was already zipped up. He took the hint, quietly entering his tent and zipping it. As he lay in his sleeping bag, hearing her breathing a few meters away from him, his eyes watered. It wasn't supposed to be like this.

Chapter 9

Zephyra lay in her tent, listening to the sounds of nature around her. It was the first time she'd been camping since she was a small child. When she and Noah had been talking about it, she'd always imagined they'd stay up late together, maybe even share a tent so she wouldn't feel alone. Instead, now she was so angry at him—she wanted to kill him.

She should have been exhausted after their long ride. Long dead to the world. There were faint snores travelling around her from other sleepers, but she was wired awake. She'd seen Noah at dinner, having the time of his life, with Felicia hanging off his arm. Boys never had to suffer when things like that happened. He had a boner, but she, as the object of his boner was looked down upon. She could see the boy's eyes watching her, wondering what she did to make him get a boner.

After tossing and turning into the early hours of the morning, she fell asleep.

'Zephyra, Zephyra.' Someone was shaking her awake.

She blinked her eyes open, feeling like someone had beaten her.

'It's time to wake up.' Noah was crouching next to her sleeping bag. 'Here. I got you a coffee and breakfast.'

She gratefully took the coffee from him, taking a sip. He'd added three sugars and a half milk, just the way she liked it. She took the plate of toast he was holding out and ate it slowly.

He sat on the floor beside her. 'How did you sleep?'

'Shit,' she said, her voice gravelly.

'Yeah, me too.' He held his hands across his knees and looked down at them. 'I'm really sorry about what happened yesterday.' He glanced up quickly and back down. 'I didn't mean to embarrass you.'

Her heart softened. She wanted to be angry at him, but he looked like a little boy and her rancour was fading.

'Um, how did I end up across your lap?' she asked.

'I was trying to stop your head from hitting into the window.'

'Oh.' She remembered the pain in her temple. She must have banged it while she was napping.

'Do you forgive me?'

She nodded.

He smiled, his blue eyes crinkling. Something happened to her stomach.

Felicia peered through the tent. 'You'd better hurry, Zephyra. Everyone has already packed up.'

Zephyra gulped the last of her coffee. Noah took the cup and plate and stood. She unzipped her sleeping bag and got out. Noah looked down at her, his eyes nodding approvingly. She was wearing a singlet top and shorts, the tops of her breast visible above the straps.

'I need to get dressed.'

Noah nodded, his eyes still on her top.

She glanced down and could see the outline of an erection in his lycra shorts. 'Get out.' Zephyra snapped.

Noah blinked, flushing. 'Sorry.'

Felicia was standing by the door. If he left now, she'd wonder what she was doing in here again. 'You stay. I'll go change in the toilets.' She snatched up her backpack and stomped out of her tent.

What the hell was going on with Noah? When did he become such a horn dog where his dick was constantly getting hard? Adolescent boys were so revolting. Like dogs in heat. Was he always like this or was this a recent phenomenon? No, she would have noticed. *It's the lycra,* darling, her mother's voice drawled in her head. *It hides no sins.*

He was such a pig. She couldn't believe she had been ready to forgive him.

When she returned, Noah was packing up her tent, Felicia helping him. 'We're nearly done.' Felicia beamed at her. 'Noah is so good with his hands. He put the tent down in three motions.' Felicia looked at him with admiration.

'Oh, he's something alright,' Zephyra muttered.

Noah glanced at her from the corner of his eyes and quickly away.

'I'll take over from here.' She snatched her tent from his hands.

'Could you give us a minute?' Noah asked Felicia.

Felicia nodded, her eyes wide like a puppy dog. 'I'll meet you at the bikes.' She sauntered away, her hips swaying it what was obviously an exaggerated motion.

Did Felicia like Noah? There was no accounting for taste.

Noah turned toward her. 'Listen, I'm sorry it keeps happening.' He rubbed the back of his nap. 'It's only because of how I feel about—'

'It's gross.' she cut him off, squishing my sleeping bag into the carry bag.

'It's natural—'

'You're like a dog in heat, constantly having a boner,' Zephyra muttered.

'That's mean. I'm just a regular teenage boy.'

'You mean a regular, horny teenager?'

'Yes, I'm a regular guy. It's a regular thing. It's only gross because of your romance novels.'

'Yeah, they don't go around with a constant boner that they want to poke girls with.'

'That's because they're not real men. They're fictional.' Noah shouted.

'Well, I prefer not real men than to be dealing with this.' She pointed at him.

'So you're never going to be interested in dating?' Noah asked.

'Not a boy my age.'

He paused. It looked like he was about to say something, but then thought better of it. 'Okay, so that's that.'

'What's what?'

'Nothing, absolutely nothing. I'm glad we got that all cleared up.' He walked off to Felicia.

They rode for the rest of the day. Usually he'd be trying to match her ride, coming back for her, keeping tabs on her. Today, he just rode ahead with the fray. Zephyra was one of the last ones to pull up. He was already in the shower. She saw his tent. It was next to Felicia and Terry. He hadn't left a space for her. Maybe it was best. They probably needed a break from each other.

During dinner, she sat on the edge of the table. Noah and Felicia were in the centre, talking to each other. They were in each other's faces. Felicia kept touching his shoulder. Zephyra was talking to Lisa, one of her teammates, and when she looked back, they were gone.

'Do you want to go for a walk?' Lisa asked.

Zephyra shook her head. 'I'm just going to find a quiet place to read.'

She went to her tent and took out her romance novel. They were camping at another caravan park and there was a bench by the river with a light above it. A perfect place to read. She needed some solitude. She wasn't used to having people around her all day.

She walked to the bench and sat down, opening her novel. Within a few pages, she felt the familiar calm settling over her as she disappeared into the historical romance world and became her heroine. She loved the escapism of it. She heard a murmur of voices and looked around. There was someone in the trees to the left. It sounded like Noah. She put her book down and walked toward the trees. Peering through, she saw his back. He was kissing Felicia, whose back was against the tree. Felicia was gripping his back tightly, while his hands were holding her waist. His head bent and he nuzzled her neck before moving down to her breasts, his hands kneading them. They were so into each other, whispered sighs and murmurs, travelling across the night. Somehow, Noah looked so manly—the way he was kissing her, the way she was responding.

Anger coursed through her. How could he? Oh my God. What was she feeling? Was she jealous of him kissing Felicia? Zephyra took a step forward, and a branch broke under her foot. She gasped, ducking down.

'Is someone there?' Felicia asked.

Zephyra crawled into the bushes and away, keeping to the shadows so they couldn't see her. She returned to her tent and zipped herself in, realising there were tears on her cheek. What was she feeling?

That night she slept, dreams tormenting her. In those, it wasn't Felicia that Noah was kissing; it was her. He was wearing a Scottish kilt, like Jamie, in the book she was reading. He was kissing her hard, his hands all over her body. Zephyra woke up with her hands cupping herself. She ducked her hand into panties, touching herself, thinking about Noah as ecstasy swept her. Her eyes snapped open? What was happening? Did she desire Noah?

Chapter 10

NOAH

Felicia found him after his conversation with Zephyra. He'd been standing by the river, leaning against a tree, feeling sorry for himself, hiding his tears. When he heard branches snapping behind him, he'd been hoping it was Zephyra coming to apologise. Instead, Felicia approached in denim cutoffs and a pink spaghetti top strap. The sun had tanned her arms and legs and she looked glamourous.

'What are you doing here by yourself?' she'd asked, approaching him with a smile.

'Just enjoying the river.'

She came to stand beside him and they'd both looked out at the river flowing in front of him.

'What are you thinking about?' She'd looked at him with concern.

He'd shrugged.

'Did you and Zephyra have a fight?' she'd asked.

He'd nodded, the words climbing to his throat before he'd thought it through. 'Do you think I'm gross?'

'What?' She'd looked at him with surprise.

'Zephyra said teenage boys are gross.' He'd tried to give her background.

'Some teenage boys are, but you definitely are not. You are the opposite of gross.' She'd looked at his chest in admiration.

He'd felt his back straighten. This was the first time a girl had looked at him with such open appreciation. He didn't know what to do about it? Each time he'd tried to kiss Zephyra, she'd flinched and shut him down. He'd wanted to reach for Felicia, but was too scared she'd rebuff him. What if he wasn't reading her signals right?

'You really think so?' he'd asked, trying to keep the conversation going so he could figure out if she really liked him.

'Oh, yeah. You are fine.' She'd touched his bicep and gently squeezed.

He'd leaned up against the tree as she moved toward him. He gingerly placed his hands on her waist, waiting to see if she'd throw them off. She'd stepped closer, her breasts pressing up against his chest, her arms moving around his neck. She was much smaller than him and he bent his knees. He didn't know who made the move first, but somehow they moved in sync—he moving his head down, her on her tippy-toes. They'd kissed, her lips soft against his, her body curvy, her smell sweet. He'd gotten hard, prodding into her, and tensed, expecting her to recoil and push him away. Instead, she'd ground her hips against his, grabbed him tighter. Did she like it? He'd lost all thoughts, completely caught up in the moment and in the feel of her in his arms. It was only when Felicia thought someone was watching them that the spell between them broke.

Noah had walked Felicia back to their tent, feeling like a million bucks.

He took his backpack and went to the bathroom block. He'd already had a shower after his ride, but he needed some release. Being with Felicia had stirred up his feelings. He ducked into the cubicle, closing the door as he masturbated. As he closed his eyes and relived the moments with Felicia, her warm body against his, her breasts under his hands. Suddenly, her face changed, and it was Zephyra he was kissing. Zephyra's breasts he was touching. After he'd cleaned himself off with tissues, he stepped out and brushed his teeth. He needed to get over Zephyra. He'd spent four years pining for her, hoping and praying that one day she would feel the same way. That their friendship would become more. She'd made her feelings clear. She found him gross. He needed to put her in the past.

He walked out of the toilets, deep in thought, and stepped against someone.

'Ouch.' Zephyra said, dropping her toiletry bag.

'Sorry. I didn't see you.' He bent and picked it up. 'Are you okay?'

'Yes.' She was rubbing her foot. 'Fine. Just a little sore.'

'Okay.' He stepped away, feeling weirdly uncomfortable and guilty, as if she knew he was thinking about her as he pleasured himself. 'Good night.' Noah walked off, expecting to hear her footsteps behind him. He looked over his shoulder. She was limping, her face grimacing in pain. Shit, he'd hurt her. He walked back. 'How badly did I hurt you?' He bent to check her foot. She was wearing slippers. He was wearing boots and there was a red mark on her foot.

'I'm fine.'

'No, you're not.' He stood, looking around. There was a common room, and he'd seen a kitchen there. There would be a fridge with ice, or even a first aid kit. He picked Zephyra up and walked with her.

Her eyes widened, and she yelped, grasping hold of his shoulders. 'What are you doing?'

'We'll get some ice to for you.'

'I don't need you to carry me. I'm okay.'

'It's just a short distance. Anyway, I can barely feel you.' Noah purposely kept his gaze straight ahead, not looking down at her again. He stepped into the common area and placed her on the couch. He rifled through the cupboards and found the first aid kit, taking out an ice pack that he activated and placed it on her foot. 'How does it feel?' he asked.

She winced. 'Better.'

He lifted it and looked. It seemed red, but there wasn't much swelling. 'I don't think it's too bad. We'll hold the ice for ten minutes and see how it feels after that.'

Silence descended as he held the ice pack to her foot.

'It doesn't feel that bad,' Zephyra said. 'I think it will be fine in a little while.'

He nodded, relieved.

'Here. I can take over.' She put her foot on her bent knee and held the ice pack to it.

He stepped back, sat on the sofa across from her.

'You can go to bed. I'll be fine.'

He shook his head. 'I'll help you back to your tent. Make sure you're sorted for the night.'

'Thanks.'

He nodded. The silence stretched out.

'So you and Felicia, huh?'

He looked up at her. 'Is it that obvious?'

'Only to me, because I know you so well.'

Her voice sounded weird. Was she blushing? He remembered the branch snapping, Felicia's insistence that someone had been watching them. Did Zephyra spy on them?

'I didn't realise you were into her.' Her hand clenched on the ice pack, the crackle filling the silence.

The devil prodded him. He leaned back and crossed his arms. 'You know what the song says, "Love the one you're with." It's good to be with someone who doesn't think teenage boys are gross.'

Zephyra flushed, her eyes fluttering away from his. She had definitely been spying on them.

'Don't you think it's mean to be with someone who likes you, if you don't like them?'

'Who says I don't like her? I like her just fine.' Noah smiled as he remembered the feel of Felicia's soft breasts beneath his hands.

'Do you like her, or just her boobs?' Zephyra demanded.

She wiped the smile off his face. It was like she was reading his mind. 'I like her just fine.'

'Okay, so does she have a brother or a sister?'

Noah searched his brain, trying to think about one thing he knew about Felicia. They'd never really spoken at school about anything personal, just about school stuff when they were in the same class. Wait a minute, why did he have to justify himself to Zephyra? 'Why, you jealous?'

'No, of course not,' she snapped.

He looked at her closer. Shit! He'd just been stirring her, but her retort sounded like he'd hit a nerve. What should he do? He'd only hooked up with Felicia because he thought there was no chance with Zephyra. Should he cool it with Felicia and try with Zephyra again?

'How's your foot?' he asked, wanting to change the subject.

Zephyra looked down, wiggling her toes. 'Much better.' She tossed the icepack into the rubbish bin.

He bent and picked her up. 'I'll take you to your tent.'

'I can walk,' she said breathily, wrapping her arms around his neck.

He smiled. Her words said one thing, but her body another. She enjoyed being carried.

He reached her tent, and gently placed her on the ground, purposely keeping his arms around her torso so she hung in the air, pressed up against him. She looked at him and he saw it, a quick flash of desire, before she tamped it down. He slid her down, letting her feet gently land on the ground.

There was a footstep to the left, and Felicia appeared out of the darkness. 'Noah,' she called.

'Hey, Felicia.' He stepped away from Zephyra. 'I was just helping Zephyra because she hurt her foot.' He went to her and curved his arm around Felicia's waist, leaning down and kissing her hard. He wasn't ready to let Zephyra off the hook yet. If she wanted him, she was going to have to show it properly, rather than have him stop everything for her.

'Goodnight, Zephyra,' he said, not looking at her as he walked Felicia back to his tent. 'Tell me about your family?' he asked, loud enough so that Zephyra could hear him. He was going to show her he liked more than Felicia's boobs.

Chapter 11

Zephyra spent the night tossing and turning. Noah had awakened something inside her, something she didn't know existed. She kept thinking about his large hands, the way he carried her, took care of her so tenderly. When he'd walked away with Felicia so casually, she'd felt so lost. She was used to commanding his attention.

Was there a part of her that had always known that he was more into her than she was into him? A part of her that had enjoyed being held up on a pedestal and now that he'd moved on, she felt lost. She'd taken him for granted, but now it was too late. He was with Felicia.

As they rode that day, she tried to push away the thoughts, but she kept replaying images of their years together. Her fourteenth birthday when her mother abandoned her to go away with a new boyfriend. Noah had invited her to his house. His mother had helped him prepare a small dinner party. They'd put up decorations, bought her favourite cake—red velvet, and had a birthday message written on it. In her fifteenth year, she'd gotten the flu. Her mother was in a new relationship and showed up every second day with groceries, but otherwise left Zephyra to her own devices. It was Noah who went to the video store and got her DVDs to watch. He borrowed books and magazines from the library. Brought her home-cooked meals from home.

When she thought of every major occasion, he was always there, taking care of her. She'd always taken it for granted. Even when she'd been undecided about coming on the bike ride, he understood and respected her choice. She hit the pedals hard, wanting to hurt herself as she remembered the way she'd called him gross after the incident on the bus. He'd been so hurt. She'd behaved like such a mean girl, no better than all the kids who bullied him. The tears dried on her face as she rode.

At the end of the ride, she pulled up. Felicia and Noah were already at the refreshment table, arm in arm. Noah waved at her as she got off, but didn't walk over to talk to her and check on her. He was now caring for Felicia. Instead, he brought Felicia a bottle of water.

Zephyra tramped to the refreshment tent and got herself a bottle of water, turning away from them as she drank.

After her shower, she went to the barbecue. Felicia and Noah were sitting side by side, their heads together. Zephyra was getting sausages when she heard someone calling her name. Noah waved her over as she turned to find him. She reluctantly walked over.

'We saved you a seat.' Noah pointed to the chair opposite.

She wanted to refuse, but then she'd look churlish. 'Thanks.' She sat and started eating, shoving her sausage into her mouth. The sooner she ate, the quicker she could leave.

'I am so sore,' Felicia said, rubbing her thighs. 'I started cramping like crazy that last five kilometres. Thankfully, Noah gave me a deep heat massage when we came back.' She kissed Noah on the cheek. 'He's the best.'

Zephyra nodded, clamping her mouth around the food.

'How's your foot?' Noah asked.

'Good. Good.' Zephyra lied. It had been throbbing the last few kilometres.

Noah frowned, but said nothing. Felicia dominated the conversation, and they were both content to leave her to it.

Afterwards, Zephyra forced herself to walk without limping, even though her foot was killing her. She didn't want Noah feeling sorry for her anymore. She walked away from everyone and into the woods and called her mother.

'Zephyra, how is the bike riding going? It was such a great thing you went. Lee and I have had our second honeymoon. With the house to ourselves, we're just able to relax and go with the flow,' her mother continued, without giving her a chance to answer.

'Oh, great,' Zephyra said, taken aback. She'd expected to hear there was trouble in paradise, not that her presence was apparently the mood-killer. 'It's going great here, too. I just think I hurt my foot—'

Zephyra heard Lee in the background. 'Sue, we need more beer.'

'I've got to go. We'll talk tomorrow.' Her mother hung up the phone.

Zephyra held the phone to her ear, her eyes tearing. She was going to ask her mother to come pick her up. Her foot was getting tender, and she didn't know if she could keep going. Somehow, since Noah had cut her out, everything was so much harder. She couldn't concentrate the way she did before on the ride. She just kept dwelling on all the things that were bringing her down.

She heard a crack of branches behind her and quickly wiped her face. She half turned, checking to see who it was. A large man loomed out of the woods and her heart stuttered to a stop. The man stepped into the light and she saw it was Noah. How was it he had transformed into this hulk of a man overnight?

'I was looking for you,' Noah said, approaching her. 'Wanted to see how your foot is going.'

'Great. I'm fine.'

He stood next to her, looking from the phone to her face. 'Did you call Sue?'

She shrugged, not saying anything. It was kind of annoying how in tune with her he was.

'Talking to her usually puts you in a mood.' He paused, letting the silence settle on them.

If it was anyone else, she'd feel the need to fill it with meaningless chatter, but with Noah it was natural to just stand there and stare out at the moon.

'Can you believe how beautiful the country night is?' He looked up at the moon hanging above the forest before them, like a beautiful pendant. The stars were so bright and it was balmy.

'Yeah, it really is.' She sighed, feeling the magic of the night relaxing her.

'Can I check your foot?' Noah asked.

Zephyra shook her head. She knew if he saw it, he'd know how bad it was.

'Or I can tell Mr Brent that you hurt it and he can come look.'

Zephyra groaned. 'Seriously.'

'Seriously.'

'Fine.' She plopped on the ground.

Noah kneeled before her. He took off her slipper and sock. She winced. He lifted his phone and turned on the torch function. Her foot was now mottled and bruised.

'Shit. This is bad.'

She sighed. She knew it was bad.

'I'm just going to press on it, make sure no bones were broken.' He did a first aid course as part of his scout training and was always the go to for nicks and grazes. He squeezed it and she moaned gently. 'It's not broken, but I don't think you can ride on it tomorrow.'

She nodded. She'd already reached that conclusion.

'Maybe you should—' He cut himself off before finishing as he looked at her phone. 'You know, I've been feeling a bit off, too. I'm thinking about calling my dad to come pick me up tomorrow.'

Zephyra's eyes teared. He'd realised that she'd tried asking Sue to come pick her up, only to be blown off. Now he was making an excuse to get her home.

'You're such a good friend.' She squeezed his hand. 'I'm sorry I've taken you for granted.'

He looked down at her hands before sitting down beside her, his arm over her shoulders. She curled into him and cried, feeling sorry for herself. Why did her mother never put her first? She thought she'd dealt with her trauma and processed it, but she was feeling so tired and so sore, she couldn't push it away.

'It'll be okay. I'll talk to Mr Brent. You can ride in the emergency car tomorrow and hopefully a day's rest will improve your foot.'

Zephyra nodded, wiping her face. There was nothing for it. She would have to endure. She yawned.

'Let's get you to bed.' Noah stood and tugged her up next to him. He went to pick her up, but she pushed him away.

'Just help me walk.' He nodded. Holding out his arm and they slowly hobbled back to camp.

As they broke through the woods, Felicia was there. 'I was looking for you everywhere Noah,' she snapped, inspecting the way Noah was propping Zephyra up against him, practically carrying her.

'Zephyra's foot is worse. Can you get Mr Brent so we can talk to him?'

Felicia hesitated, not happy about leaving them alone, before doing as he asked. Ten minutes later, Mr Brent came with a first aid kit. He examined Zephyra's foot and concluded she couldn't ride.

'Zephyra's hoping one day's rest will help her feel better and then she can resume,' Noah covered for her. 'Can she be in the follow car?'

Mr Brent nodded. 'I think that will be fine.'

Chapter 12

NOAH

After Noah left Zephyra at her tent, he walked across the field. Felicia was waiting for him by his tent.

'How is Zephyra?' Felicia asked.

'Good. She'll be in the provisions truck.'

'She really should go home if she's hurt.'

'It's not that bad,' he said, not wanting to tell her about Sue flaking out. 'She just needs a day's rest.'

'I don't know. It looked pretty bad to me. Even Mr Brent said she should go home.'

'She's fine.' Noah snapped. He didn't want Zephyra to go home. They were finally turning a corner. His head was reeling from her admission that she had taken him for granted. It was working. His dreams were coming true. She was seeing him as something more than just a friend.

Felicia stepped up to him, wound her arms around his neck. 'You're such a good friend,' she murmured, kissing him on the lips. 'I'm so lucky to have you as a boyfriend.'

As Noah kissed her, guilt pinged inside of him. This was wrong. He didn't feel the same way about Felicia that she felt about him. Their first kiss had been so whirlwind, and then he'd continued it, because of Zephyra's reaction. But they'd spent the past 24 hours in each other's company and in between make out sessions, he'd tried to have a conversation with her, only to find she was only interested in talking about getting her nails done or how much she loved the Kardashians. They just didn't gel together. There was no natural flow to the conversation, and their sense of humour didn't mesh.

Felicia's hands moved down his chest and to his groin. Each time they made out, they got more and more physical, which he'd been into, but now he wondered if that was the best idea.

He took Felicia's hand and stopped her.

'What is it?' Felicia looked at him suspiciously.

He didn't know what to do. He still liked Felicia, but he wasn't sure if he should pursue this. But then again, was he just thinking this because Zephyra had given him a glimmer of hope?

'I'm just tired,' he said in the end. This wasn't a conversation or decision he wanted to make right now. He needed some time to process and see how he really felt.

'Really?' Felicia looked at him suspiciously. 'I have an idea.' She tiptoed her hands on his chest. 'Why don't we bunk together tonight in one tent? That way, we can sleep and still be together.'

'Oh, that's not a good idea. Mr Brent forbid that from happening.'

'What he doesn't know...' Felicia opened his tent and took her sleeping bag from hers into his. 'We'll just join these together and we'll be fine.'

Noah hesitated, not sure what to do. He was tempted. Felicia bent over, the thought of them being together all night. But he also knew where this would lead to. If they continued the way they were going, they would go too far and there would be no way back. He had the condoms still in his backpack, tormenting him. He didn't owe Zephyra anything. She was the one who didn't want to be with him. If he and Felicia took things to the next level, then that was their business. But was it fair to take things to the next level with Felicia, when he was getting the sense that this was just a temporary situation?

He thought of his father, thinking with his dick and leaving messy circumstances behind him. Is that who he wanted to be?

'No, I don't think it's a good idea. I think we should be in our own tents.' He bent and took her sleeping bag and put it back into her tent.

'Are you changing your mind about us? I thought you liked me, but now that Zephyra is needy, you're not interested in me.'

'No, that's not what's happening. Zephyra and I are friends. I just don't want us to rush into anything. If this is something more, then we need to give it time to develop.'

'Do you really believe that, or are you just waiting to dump me?'

'No, I really believe that. We just need to spend more time together, get to know each other more.'

'You're so sweet.' She wrapped her arms around his neck. 'You're not like other boys who are only interested in sex. Like my ex. He was just interested in one thing.'

He'd suspected that she was more experienced than he was. The way she'd moved her way around his body, and now he had it confirmed. There was a sinking feeling in his stomach. He wanted to be with someone who thought it would be special, too.

After she left, he zipped the entrance to his tent. He needed a time out to see what he really felt. He closed his eyes and was under.

The next day, he packed up his tent quickly and walked to Zephyra's tent, Felicia watching him plaintively.

Zephyra was packing up her sleeping bag, her movements slow and deliberate. She had dark circles under her eyes.

'Did you get any sleep? Were you in pain?' he asked, taking the heavy backpack from her.

'No, it wasn't the foot.' She sat on the ground.

'Sue?' he asked.

She nodded quickly.

He hated how her mother destroyed her so quickly. Noah clasped her shoulder before rolling up her bag and clamping her tent together. He walked with her to the bus and placed her back on the trailer with her tent and backpack. They went to breakfast, the two of them falling into a peaceful rhythm together. Felicia joined them.

'You're so lucky having Noah help you pack up. It took me ages on my own,' Felicia said.

'I'm lucky that he's a good friend.'

'I'm lucky too. He's a great boyfriend.' Felicia pulled him down for a kiss. He kept himself stiff, letting her kiss his lips, his cheeks flushing, feeling uncomfortable with Zephyra there. When he broke off the kiss, he looked at Zephyra. She was looking down at her breakfast, not paying attention.

After breakfast, he walked Zephyra to the bus and made sure she was on. When he was riding it usually focused him, but today he didn't care about achieving his personal best. He kept to the back, regularly dropping to Zephyra's window. Felicia dropped back with him. Watching him sullenly as he did a did a dab on the bike, making Zephyra laugh as he rode without using his arms.

When they came to the next stop, he was one of the last ones to arrive. Felicia was waiting, arms crossed sullenly.

'Where were you?' she demanded.

'I rode at the back. I wanted to keep an eye on Zephyra.'

'Really. So she's more important than your girlfriend.'

He gaped, unsure how to respond. Felicia stomped off. He was relieved, aware of the fact that she was making a scene.

He walked to the bus and helped Zephyra off. 'How are you feeling today?' he asked.

'Much better.' She looked down at her foot. 'I think I'll be able to ride tomorrow.' She smiled.

'Great. I'll help you set up your tent.' He walked with her and quickly put up her tent, before setting his own up.

Felicia stomped up to them, putting her tent next to his. Feeling guilty, he helped her put up the tent. She seemed placated by him making boyfriend overtures.

Zephyra walked to the bathroom and Felicia helped him unpack his stuff into his tent. She unzipped the pouch in his backpack and yanked out the condoms. 'Oh, you prepared?' She smiled with delight.

'No, I didn't — I had those—'

'I like a man who prepares.' She hugged him tight.

Zephyra came back and Felicia tucked the condoms in his pants pocket. 'Keep those for later.'

Shit, how was he going to explain that he didn't get those for them?

At dinner, Felicia sat between him and Zephyra. 'Are you going to ride tomorrow?' she asked Zephyra.

Zephyra nodded.

'Are you sure you're up to it? Maybe you should go home?'

'I'll be fine,' Zephyra muttered, stabbing her salad.

Felicia stuck to him all night, acting like she was glued to his side. She kept interjecting into his conversation with Zephyra. He realised he'd made her feel insecure by not riding with her the way he did a few days before. The more demanding she was, the more he was turned off.

The decision was being made for him. It was time to break it off. He'd have to wait until the bike ride finished. He did not want to deal with an awkward ex for the next few days. In the meantime, he just needed to keep her at a distance, so she got the sense that it wasn't on. He was relieved Zephyra's tent was next to them. Hopefully, it would make Felicia more bashful about trying anything.

Chapter 13

Zephyra woke up to loud voices coming from her left. She heard Noah shouting, 'This isn't a good idea!'

'Why? If we're boyfriend and girlfriend, then this is what we should do.'

There was the sound of nylon rustling, kissing sounds. OMG, Felicia was in Noah's tent and they were doing it. Zephyra covered her ears with her pillow. She sought her headphones and phone, putting them in. She did not want to listen to them having sex. This was horrific. She hunkered down, eventually falling asleep.

In the morning, Noah was putting his tent down when she woke up, Felicia next to him, working on her tent.

'Good morning,' Zephyra said.

'It sure is.' Felicia sashayed.

Felicia went to put something in her backpack and it fell open. 'Whoops,' she laughed, picking up the condoms. 'You'd better take these left-overs.'

Zephyra looked at Noah. He looked at the condoms, horrified.

'They're not mine,' he yelped.

'You brought them on the trip, didn't you? And how lucky you got to use them.'

Noah looked at her guiltily.

Zephyra turned away, rolling up her sleeping bag. She glanced over her shoulder and saw Felicia leaving with her packed tent and sleeping bag.

'I need to explain,' Noah said, after Felicia left.

'You don't owe me any explanations. You're a free man, free to do whatever you like.'

Zephyra walked past him, avoiding him during breakfast.

Later, as they prepared to start the ride, Noah was with his bike, Felicia nowhere to be seen. Zephyra got on her bike and Noah shadowed her, remaining in the back as everyone overtook them.

'I'm okay. You can go on ahead and catch up to Felicia.'

'I'm right where I want to be.' Noah continued cycling next to her.

Soon, their regular relationship settled. He would make a goofy pose and make her laugh. They'd do short sprints and then relax. It was nice just being in the groove together, being friends. That's all they were. She'd missed her chance. He was now with Felicia. She needed to respect that and just appreciate his friendship. If she had a time machine, she would have done things differently.

After dinner, he set up his tent next to hers.

'Where's Felicia?' she asked.

Noah shrugged.

It was on the tip of her tongue to ask if there was trouble in paradise, but she snatched them back. It wasn't her business.

'It's our last night,' Noah said.

Zephyra smiled.

It was a blustery night. The rain began. They retreated into their sleeping bags. She was lying down when water began leaking from the roof. 'You have got to be kidding me,' she exclaimed, getting up and putting on her clothes and jacket.

'Is everything okay?' Noah called out from his tent.

'Yep. All good.' She lay back and closed her eyes, trying to sleep. A drop fell into her eye. Soon her sleeping bag was damp. 'Fuck, fuck, fuck.' She lost it.

'I'm heading over,' Noah called out. She heard rustling outside and the zipper of her tent opened. Noah's face appeared. 'What's wrong?' He was holding a torch in his hand, which he flashed into the room. 'Shit. Okay, come into my tent.'

She groaned and threw her belongings into the backpack, and walked barefoot through the damp grass to Noah's tent.

'We'll have to bunk together.' He opened his sleeping bag up and lay it flat on the floor. 'Lucky for us, my mother packed an extra blanket.' He threw it on top of the sleeping bag. Then got a t-shirt and folded it up so that it was a pillow. He lay down and patted it next to her.

She lay down next to him, covering herself up with a blanket. It was suddenly awkward, lying so close to him. Noah turned off the torch, and they were in darkness. He was lying pressed up against her. She was so aware of her hands. Didn't know where to put them.

'Are you okay?' he whispered in the darkness, just above her left ear.

'I'm good,' she whispered back, gripping the blanket tightly to her chest. 'What would Felicia think about this? She might get the wrong idea?'

'It's not her business.'

'So you just used her for sex and dumped her?'

'Why would you think that about me? I'm not like my father.' He snapped on the torch again, leaning up on his elbow and looking down at her.

'I heard you both last night. I saw the condoms.'

'If you heard us last night, then you know what happened.'

'No, I put my headphones on and blocked it out. I didn't want to listen to you having sex.'

'And what makes you so sure that we had sex?'

'I know what sex sounds like. And Felicia told me.'

'So Felicia told you we had sex, and I told you we didn't, but you believe her.'

'Oh, come on. Are you saying that you had a girl all hot and bothered for you and you turned her down?'

'So that's what you think about me. That I'm no better than a dog in heat.' He leaped over her. 'I need a breather. I'm going to the toilet.' He unzipped the tent and stomped out.

'Noah, don't go.' She saw tears in his eyes and felt guilty. She didn't mean to hurt his feelings. By the time he returned, she was droopy. 'Can we talk?' she asked.

'I'm tired. We'll talk tomorrow.' He lay down, turning his back to her. They pressed their backs up against each other. She was relieved to have his warmth.

She woke up surrounded by warmth, nestled into Noah's chest, her arm over his waist, his arm under hers. She wanted to lie here forever. The moment he came to, she felt a change in his breathing. His eyes fluttered open, and he looked at her, his blue eyes so full of happiness. She felt floaty seeing the joy on his face.

'I believe you,' Zephyra said, brushing his hair out of his eyes.

'About what?' he asked.

She reached up and tugged his head toward her. 'That you didn't have sex with Felicia?'

He smiled. His lips were about to touch hers when he pulled back. 'We can't do this.' He got up and got dressed.

'What?' she asked. 'Why not?'

He didn't speak, just got dressed quickly and left the tent.

She was packing up her tent, tears in her eyes. What had happened? She thought they were finally at a point where they were admitting everything, and then he stormed off.

She was packing up her tent when Noah returned, a big smile on his face.

'What are you doing here?' she snapped, crabby at seeing him so happy.

He put his arms around her waist and pulled her to him. 'Now we can start the day properly.' He leaned down to kiss her.

She hit him in the chest and pulled away. 'Now you want to kiss me?'

'I had to end things with Felicia before we could officially start anything. I'm not my father.'

She smiled, wrapping her arms around his neck. 'I'm so happy.' They kissed. It was like a romance novel come true. As their lips touched, the world receded, and she was filled with longing and desire. She couldn't believe it took her so long to realise that Noah was the one.

He lifted his head, his eyes heavy-lidded. 'That was worth the wait.'

She slapped his arm and laughed. They walked together arm in arm with their bikes.

Chapter 14

Noah sat on the bus, Zephyra's head on his shoulder as they lolled lazily on the drive back home. He was so content. The trip had been everything he'd ever wanted; he and Zephyra were finally together. He sighed to himself.

'You okay?' Zephyra asked, looking up at him.

'Happy.' He smiled as he intertwined their hands together and held them in his lap.

'Me too.'

Noah leaned his head back, catching sight of Felicia who was giving him daggers. He sunk deeper into his seat, disrupting Zephyra.

She looked up. 'Felicia?' she asked.

Noah nodded. He hated that he'd hurt Felicia. He'd genuinely liked her, it's just that he loved Zephyra. His arms tightened around Zephyra. She sighed happily against his chest.

'She'll get over it. Anyway, she should be the one apologising for lying,' Zephyra said harshly.

'I know.' Noah said, even though he wasn't sore at Felicia about lying that they'd had sex. Whenever he remembered her distraught face when he'd rebuffed her in his tent, a sinking feeling of guilt hit him.

Felicia's eyes had pooled with tears. 'You think I'm a slut,' she'd uttered, her voice breaking.

'No, of course not.' Noah had wiped her tears, then shifted her off his lap and next to him. 'I just want it to be special the first time. With someone I have feelings for.'

'You mean with Zephyra?' Felicia had asked, her eyes narrowing.

Noah had shifted uneasily, words stuck in his throat.

'Am I just a stepping stone to you and Zephyra getting together?' Felicia asked.

'No, no. I like you. I just want to take it slow,' Noah had reassured her.

He would always regret not breaking it off then and there. Instead, he'd found her a few hours afterwards, when he and Zephyra had admitted their feelings. Felicia was packing her tent and had greeted him with a smile, which quickly faded as soon as she saw his flushed face and that he was cracking his knuckles as he'd approached.

'I don't think this is working out,' Felicia had said, turning her back to him as she'd folded up her sleeping bag. 'I think it's best if we break it off now.'

He'd heard the tears in her voice.

'I'm so sorry, Felicia,' he'd said. He'd waited a beat, but she didn't turn around. He'd hurried away, wanting to at least give her privacy.

Now, he rested his head against the bus headrest and closed his eyes, focussing on the good feelings.

When they arrived back at school an hour later, he and Zephyra remained on the bus, disembarking last. He wanted to give Felicia a head start.

Noah collected his things, looking around the empty car park. His parents had told him they'd be at school, waiting for him.

Zephyra put on her backpack and sat on her bike. 'You coming?' she asked.

'Of course.' He smiled and followed her, pushing away his concern.

They rode slowly home, their legs tired and sore.

'I can't wait to get into the bath,' Zephyra said, when they reached her house.

He pushed her bike under the carport and followed her into the house, carrying her backpack and tent. Her mother Sue was sitting on the couch, a sea of white tissues littering the surrounding carpet.

She looked at Zephyra with bloodshot eyes. 'He broke up with me,' she wailed, reaching her arms for her daughter.

Zephyra sighed, sitting on the couch and hugging her mother.

Noah took Zephyra's belongings into her bedroom and placed them on the floor.

'I'll call you later,' Zephyra said, blowing him a kiss over her mother's sobbing form as he walked back into the living room.

Noah nodded and rode home. When he entered, silence greeted him. 'Mum, Dad?' he called.

His sister appeared in the hallway. 'He's gone. Moved out to be with his slutty secretary.'

Noah dropped his bags with a thud. It couldn't be true. He ran into his parent's bedroom. His mother was lying on the bed, the wardrobe doors opened behind her, revealing the space where his father's clothes had once hung.

'Mum, is it true?' Noah demanded. 'Is Dad gone?'

His mother nodded faintly, still lying on the bed. Noah sat beside her. His sister stood in the doorway, her eyes red-rimmed. How could his father have done this? How could he have broken their family?

· · · ● · ● ● · · ·

Later that night he was lying in bed when his phone beeped. He looked at the screen. It was a message from Zephyra. 'I'm already missing the quiet of being out in nature.'

He hesitated, not sure whether to respond. Noah had spent the afternoon comforting his mother and stifling his own emotions. He'd called his father, who'd picked up jovially, and asked questions about Noah's trip, before cutting the call short when Noah attempted probing him about the breakup.

'I miss you,' Zephyra sent another message. 'You're the only person who gets it.'

He clenched the phone tighter in his hand. She was the only one who got it.

He typed, 'Coming over.'

He collected the tent and sleeping bag that were next to his bedroom door and left the house.

Zephyra was waiting on the porch, smiling brightly, until he was in the driveway and the porch light landed on his face, revealing his swollen eyes.

'What's wrong?' she demanded, stepping down the stairs and running toward him.

'Dad left,' he said, gutturally.

'No,' she gasped.

'Let's go to the park.' He nodded to the tent and sleeping bag on the back of his bike.

'Okay.' She ran inside, putting on her runners and a jacket.

As they glided through the dark streets, he looked through the windows of houses they passed, catching glimpses of families sitting down to dinner. That was once his home, a home full of happiness and cheer.

When they arrived at the park, they worked together in silence, setting up the tent and laying down on the sleeping bag, the entrance unzipped so they could see the full moon lighting up the sky.

'I'm sorry, Noah,' Zephyra whispered, her head on his shoulder, her arm hugging him tightly. 'Your family was like a perfect dream family. I loved going over there, having your mum make a big fuss as she served dinner.'

'I loved it too.' He blinked back the tears that seeped down his face. 'But all dreams end.' She hugged him tighter, and he felt her tear fall on his bare arm. He lifted her hand to his lips and kissed it. 'So that new dreams can begin.'

About the Author

Amra Pajalić is an award-winning author, an editor and teacher who draws on her Bosnian cultural heritage to write own voices stories for young people, who like her, are searching to mediate their identity and take pride in their diverse culture. Her short story collection *The Cuckoo's Song* (Pishukin Press, 2022) features previously published and prize-winning stories. Her debut novel *The Good Daughter*, was published by Text Publishing in 2009 and won the 2009 Melbourne Prize for Literature's Civic Choice Award and is re-released as *Sabiha's Dilemma* (Pishukin Press, 2022).

Her memoir *Things Nobody Knows But Me* (Transit Lounge, 2019) was shortlisted for the 2020 National Biography Award. She is co-editor of the anthology *Growing up Muslim in Australia* (Allen and Unwin, 2014) which was shortlisted for the 2015 Children's Book Council of the year awards. She works as a high school teacher and is completing a PhD in Creative Writing at La Trobe University.

Amra Pajalić publishes her dark fiction using pen name A. P. Pajalic. She also publishes romance novels under pen name Mae Archer.

CONNECT WITH AMRA:
www.amrapajalic.com

g goodreads.com/author/show/3310015.Amra_Pajalic

f facebook.com/AmraPajalicAuthor/

⊙ instagram.com/amrapajalicauthor/

🐦 https://twitter.com/AmraPajalic

♪ tiktok.com/@amrapajalic

▶ youtube.com/c/AmraPajalicAuthor

SIGN UP FOR AMRA'S AUTHOR NEWSLETTER

For news, giveaways, bonus material, and sneak peeks, please sign up to her newsletter below.

www.amrapajalic.com

'If you struggle to read, then
you haven't found the right
book format.'

I'm Amra Pajalić, the owner and publisher of Pishukin Press, an independent press dedicated to the publication of own voices fiction and nonfiction, as well as genre fiction.

There is a quote that states 'If you don't like to read, then you haven't found the right book.' I would like to extend that further and state that 'If you struggle to read then you haven't found the right book format.' As a high school teacher I have taught students with various individual needs and recognise the need to make books accessible for all kinds of readers. To this end I am committed to publishing all Pishukin Press titles in as many formats as possible. This includes:

Dyslexic Format Edition—printed in Dyslexic Open font in 14 point
Large Print edition—printed in Large Print Open Sans No Italics font in 18 point font size
Audiobooks AI—narrated by artificial intelligence using Google technology.
Audiobooks—narrated by performance narrators.
All books are also available in paperback and hardcover editions.

To get 10% off use discount code 10OFF

https://www.pishukinpress.com/

Sassy Saints Series

Sassy Saints Series

Follow the lives of six sassy teens coming of age in St Albans, as they navigate their sexual and cultural identity and search for belonging.

1-*Sabiha's Dilemma* (published June 2022)

Sabiha's dilemma is being the good daughter so that her mentally ill mother is accepted back into the Bosnian community.

2-*Alma's Loyalty* (October 2022)

When Alma finds out that she has a half sister she never knew, she is faced with competing loyalties.

3-*Jesse's Triumph* (January 2023)

After Jesse's debut novel is published while he's a high school student, he contends with becoming popular.

4-*Brian's Conflict* (June 2023)
Brian's dreams of being a designer are in conflict with his father's hopes he'll join the family business as a bricklayer.

5-*Dina's Burden* (September 2023)
Dina carries the burden of living up to her parent's expectations to make up for her brother's errant ways.

6-*Adnan's Secret* (December 2023)
Adnan is the perfect son carrying the weight of his migrant parent's expectations, who lives a secret life.

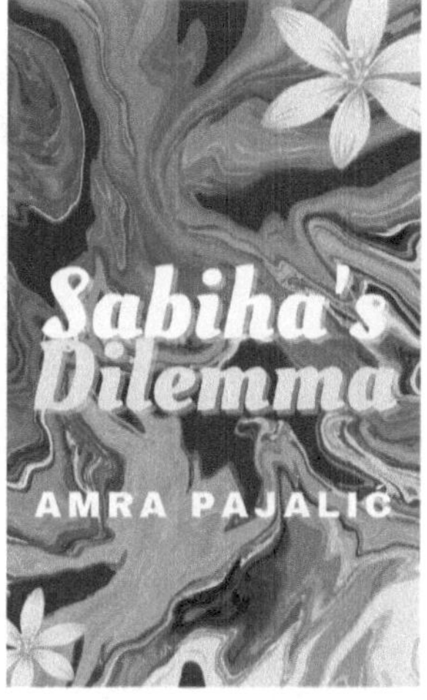

Can Sabiha play the part of the good daughter
so that her mentally ill mother is accepted back
into the Bosnian community?

Unbelievable Discounts

https://www.pishukinpress.com/

When Alma finds out that she has a half sister she never knew, she is faced with competing loyalties.

Unbelievable Discounts

https://www.pishukinpress.com/

Also by

Memoir
Things Nobody Knows But Me
Growing up Muslim in Australia

Young Adult
The Cuckoo's Song
Sabiha's Dilemma
Alma's Loyalty
The Climb

Romance as Mae Archer
Return to Me
Hollywood Dreams

Dark Fiction/Horror as A.P. Pajalic
Woman on the Edge